# Penelope
## the Foal
## Fairy

To Rowena, who loves foals

Special thanks to Rachel Elliot

Copyright © 2017 by Rainbow Magic Limited.

All rights reserved. Published by Scholastic Inc., *Publishers since 1920*. SCHOLASTIC and associated logos are trademarks and/or registered trademarks of Scholastic Inc. RAINBOW MAGIC is a trademark of Rainbow Magic Limited. Reg. U.S. Patent & Trademark Office and other countries. HIT and the HIT logo are trademarks of HIT Entertainment Limited.

The publisher does not have any control over and does not assume any responsibility for author or third-party websites or their content.

No part of this publication may be reproduced, stored in a retrieval system, or transmitted in any form or by any means, electronic, mechanical, photocopying, recording, or otherwise, without written permission of the publisher. For information regarding permission, write to Scholastic Inc., Attention: Permissions Department, 557 Broadway, New York, NY 10012.

This book is a work of fiction. Names, characters, places, and incidents are either the product of the author's imagination or are used fictitiously, and any resemblance to actual persons, living or dead, business establishments, events, or locales is entirely coincidental.

ISBN 978-1-338-20698-2

10 9 8 7 6 5 4 3 2 1     18 19 20 21 22

Printed in the U.S.A.          40
First printing 2018

# Penelope
## the Foal
## Fairy

by Daisy Meadows

SCHOLASTIC INC.

The Fairyland Palace

Farmhouse

Pond

Fluttering Fairyland Farm

Greenfields Farm

Greenfields House

Barn

Pond

Barn

Jack Frost's
Ice Castle

Wetherbury Village

Kirsty's
House

I want a farm that's just for me,
With animals I won't set free.
It's far too slow to find each one.
Let fairy magic get this done!

With magic from the fairy farm,
I'll grant my wish—to their alarm!
And if I spoil the humans' fun,
Then Jack Frost really will have won!

# Contents

# Poster Animals

"Just one day left until the farm's grand opening," said Kirsty Tate.

She was looking at a computer screen over the shoulders of Harriet and Niall Hawkins, the owners of Greenfields Farm. Her parents, Mr. and Mrs. Tate, and her best friend, Rachel Walker, were also gazing at the computer. They were

all looking at the design for the new poster that would advertise the farm.

"I feel jumpy with excitement every time I think about the grand opening tomorrow," said Rachel.

"I feel jumpy with *nervousness* every time I think about it," said Harriet with a laugh. "I can't believe there's just one day left."

"I'm sure everything will be fine," said Mr. Tate, patting Harriet's shoulder.

The Tates and Rachel were all spending spring break at Greenfields Farm, just outside Wetherbury. The Tates were friends with Harriet and Niall, and they had all been helping to get the farm ready. Tomorrow, Greenfields Farm would open to visitors for the first time, complete with a children's petting zoo.

"You've all been wonderful," said Niall, turning in his chair to smile up at them. "Especially you, Rachel and Kirsty. We were worried about being too busy to look after the baby animals this week, but you've done everything for them."

"It's been a treat to look after them," said Kirsty with a smile.

Mr. Tate was still gazing at the poster design.

"I think it needs more photos of the farm," he said.

"How about adding some photos of the baby animals?" said Rachel. "They are so cute—they'd make anyone want to visit the farm."

"Especially animal lovers like us," Kirsty added.

"We could add some photos of the foals," said Harriet. "They're really sweet—especially when they've just been groomed and are all nice and clean."

"I saw them this morning and they are definitely not clean at the moment," said Niall with a chuckle. "I've never seen such scruffy-looking foals before. Girls,  would you mind giving the foals a bath and grooming them before they have their photo taken?"

Rachel and Kirsty exchanged a glance of pure delight.

"That sounds like so much fun," said Rachel. "We'd love to do it."

"You'll need to put on your rubber boots and your oldest clothes," said Harriet. "I've found that the animals end up clean, but the people bathing them certainly don't."

Shortly afterward, the best friends were walking toward the stables, with two buckets of warm soapy water and the grooming equipment. They were wearing fraying old T-shirts and threadbare jeans, and they couldn't stop smiling.

"I think we're going to need every drop of this water," said Kirsty. "We need to get the foals clean and neat so that they look good for the posters."

"The foals are adorable, even if they are muddy," said Kirsty. "And they make such happy little neighing noises."

"Look, there's Blossom," said Rachel, spotting the cow outside her barn. "Let's go and say hello."

They hurried over, stopping to pick some juicy green grass for Blossom. She munched on it and then gave them a friendly moo.

"We're going to wash and groom the foals," Kirsty told her. "Wish us luck."

Blossom gave an extra-loud moo, which made the girls laugh. They said good-bye and then continued along the lane toward the stables. It was another sunny morning on the farm, and the air was filled with the sounds of animals all around, and the high, clear twitter of the birds.

"Everyone seems to be happy that it's springtime," said Rachel.

"*I'm* happy that it's spring vacation, and we're

spending it together," Kirsty replied, smiling at her best friend.

The girls had shared many adventures, but they never grew tired of being together. They always had lots of fun. Best of all, they had a very exciting secret, which they had never told anyone else. They were friends of Fairyland, and had met lots of fairies since they first became friends on Rainspell Island.

"Look," said Rachel as they passed the horses' paddock. "I think the horses are watching something over by the pigsty. I wonder what it could be."

Four of the horses were standing in a line with their backs to the girls. It was hard to see around them. The girls climbed up onto the paddock gate, but they still couldn't see anything.

"Let's go and check if everything's OK," said Kirsty. "If there's something wrong, we'll have to run back and tell Niall and Harriet."

They put down their buckets and brushes, and then climbed over the gate and dropped into the grassy paddock. The

horses took no notice, even when the girls walked right up next to them. Then Rachel and Kirsty saw what they were looking at.

"Oh my goodness," said Kirsty. "The foals are in the pigs' enclosure!"

"That's not all," said Rachel. "Just look at what they're *doing*!"

# A Muddy Mess

There was plenty of mud around the
pigsty. It was exactly the sort of squishy
mud that piglets love. But there wasn't
a single piglet to be seen. Instead, three
little foals with fluffy coats and long
manes were rolling around in the mud.
The girls looked around and saw another
foal jumping into a big muddy puddle

with a splash. As
they watched,
it threw
back its
head and
let out
a loud
oinking
sound.

The horses in the
paddock took a few steps backward, and
the girls exchanged a worried glance.

"The foals are acting like piglets," said
Kirsty. "Oh, Rachel, we know what this
means."

"Yes," said Rachel, looking serious. "It
means more trouble from Jack Frost and
his naughty goblins."

On the day they arrived at Greenfields

Farm, Kirsty and Rachel had met
Debbie the Duckling Fairy. She had
whisked them to the Fluttering Fairyland
Farm, a magical farm hovering among
the puffy white clouds over Fairyland.

Debbie had introduced the girls to the

other Farm Animal Fairies and their
magical baby farm animals—Splashy
the duckling, Fluffy the lamb, Frisky the
foal, and Chompy the baby goat. The
girls had been delighted to find out that
the magical animals helped the Farm
Animal Fairies look after baby farm
animals everywhere.

But as the girls were walking around
Fluttering Fairyland Farm with the
fairies and Farmer Francis, Jack Frost
and his goblins stole the fairies' magical
farm animals. Jack Frost was making
his own petting zoo at his Ice Castle,
and he wanted to fill it with lots of cute
and cuddly farm animals. He said his
pet snow goose and her baby, Snowdrop,
needed friends, so he was going to use
the fairies' magical animals to get even

more baby farm animals.

Jack Frost's plan had already caused chaos at Greenfields Farm.

"First the ducklings acted like puppies, and then the lambs behaved like kittens," said Kirsty. "Now the foals are not themselves. What are we going to do?"

Rachel glanced over at the horses again. They looked just as worried as she felt. Then she saw something out of the corner of her eye.

One of the bales of hay that were scattered around the paddock was glowing. Her heart gave a leap of excitement.

"Kirsty!" Rachel said in an eager voice. "I think there's magic happening over there."

The girls hurried over to the hay bale and kneeled down in front of it. The glow grew brighter, and the hay seemed to turn golden. Rachel and Kirsty saw it moving and reached out their hands. At once, Penelope the Foal Fairy fluttered out of the center, shaking stray strands of hay from her glittery wings.

She was wearing flowery boots with a
matching scarf wrapped around her head.
She also had on a crisp white shirt and a
skirt as blue as the sky.

"Hello, Penelope," said Kirsty. "Have
you come to help the foals?"

Penelope glanced over to where the
foals were still rolling around in the mud.
But then she shook her head.

"I wish I could help them," she said

in a soft voice. "But I can't return them to normal without Frisky. That's why I'm here. I've found out that Jack Frost has Frisky at his Ice Castle. Please, will you come with me and help me get him back?"

Rachel and Kirsty had already helped Debbie the Duckling Fairy and Elodie the Lamb Fairy get their magical animals safely back home to Fluttering Fairyland Farm. But there were still two magical animals missing, and

if they didn't come home very soon,
Greenfields Farm wouldn't be ready to
open on time. Rachel and Kirsty knew
that the fairies were depending on them.

"Of course we will," said Rachel. "We
have to get Frisky back—and fast!"

# Jack Frost's Pets

Penelope gave her wand a little flick, and a shower of pink fairy dust fluttered down around Rachel and Kirsty. They closed their eyes and felt something warm slip around their shoulders as they shrank to fairy size. Their wings unfurled and lifted them into the air. Then a blast of icy wind blew the fairy dust away.

The girls opened their eyes and found that they were flying high above the Ice Castle in Fairyland. Penelope's magic had given each of them a fluffy cape around their shoulders.

"These will keep you warm and cozy, however bitterly cold it gets," said Penelope. "My fairy magic is enough to

keep me warm."

Rachel and Kirsty shivered, feeling glad to have the capes. Jack Frost's castle was always a chilly place, but today it seemed colder than ever. There was a grim cloud looming so low that it touched the turrets.

"If Frisky is here, we'll find him," said Kirsty. "Come on, let's fly down and look around."

There were no goblins guarding the gray turrets, so the three fairies zoomed down and perched there to look into a little courtyard garden at the back of the castle. It was decorated with ice statues of animals, but there were some living

creatures there, too.

"There's the snow goose," said Rachel.

"And baby Snowdrop," Kirsty added.

"And Frisky!" cried Penelope. "Frisky is there, too!"

The three fairies shared happy smiles. It was wonderful to see Frisky again. He looked just like the foals at Greenfields Farm, except he had an extra magical sparkle. But their smiles faded when they saw that he was bumbling around the courtyard like a pig. Snowdrop, the baby snow goose, was hopping around after him, honking happily. The mother snow goose was watching them both with a puzzled expression. She was sitting beside a large brown sack. It was tied with a white rope, and it was labeled *Snow Goose Treats*.

"Even the snow goose is wondering

why Frisky isn't acting like a foal," said Kirsty.

Snowdrop and Frisky were now chasing each other around the ice statues and trying to pounce on each other. They were clearly having lots of fun.

"There's no sign of Jack Frost or the goblins," Penelope said. "Let's go and get Frisky right now."

She fluttered her wings and started to rise into the air, but Rachel put a hand on her arm to stop her.

"Hold on," she said. "We have to be careful."

As she spoke, Jack Frost hurried out into the courtyard, wearing a pair of bright-green overalls. Penelope sank down beside Rachel and Kirsty again, and they watched the Ice Lord, their hearts hammering. A few seconds later and he would have seen Penelope.

Jack Frost scooped Frisky into his bony arms and cuddled him tightly. Frisky wiggled and wriggled, trying to get away.

"Frisky doesn't like being squeezed," said Penelope.

Clinging on to the squirmy foal, Jack Frost bent down and opened the sack that the girls had seen earlier.

He pulled out a handful of something
that looked like birdseed and held it
under Frisky's snout. Frisky gave an oink,
bounded out of Jack Frost's arms, and
jumped to the ground. He aimed a hard
kick at the sack of snow goose treats, and
then darted off again.

"Come back!" Jack Frost wailed.

The mother snow goose and Snowdrop waddled over to the sack and started to nudge it with their beaks, looking up at Jack Frost with hopeful expressions. But he shook his head at them and tied up the sack.

"No," he said. "If Frisky doesn't want these, no one is having them."

# Sad Snow Geese

The snow geese waddled away, their white heads drooping a little.

"They look so sad," said Rachel.

"Poor things," Penelope said. "They chose to be Jack Frost's special pets. They really love him."

"But why is he ignoring the snow geese?" Kirsty asked.

"He's just really interested in his petting zoo now," said Penelope. "He isn't thinking about the geese."

Rachel and Kirsty looked at each other, knowing that they were both thinking the same thing. If they could get Frisky back for Penelope, maybe Jack Frost would start noticing the geese who loved him so much again.

"But how are we going to catch Frisky?" Rachel asked. "He's still darting around like a pig."

"Or being chased and cuddled by Jack Frost," said Kirsty.

She pointed to where Jack was sprinting around a frozen fountain after Frisky.

"Come here!" he roared. "Come back! I want to cuddle with you!"

He threw himself across the fountain

and managed to catch Frisky by the
back legs. Frisky oinked and wriggled as
Jack Frost picked him up.

"I've got something for you," Jack Frost
said, panting as he tried to hold on to
Frisky.

He pointed over to a small iron bench.
The fairies were startled to see a large
stuffed toy in the shape of Jack Frost.
It was sitting on the bench with its legs
crossed and a mean expression on its face.

Jack Frost clutched Frisky to his chest and carried him over to the toy. He put him down at the toy's feet.

"There," he said. "Isn't it the most beautiful thing you've ever seen?"

Frisky snorted like a pig and shrank back from Jack Frost.

"I don't think he's very impressed," said Rachel.

"Jack Frost doesn't know anything about what foals really like," Kirsty said. "He has no idea how to look after one the right way."

"But Frisky isn't acting like a foal," said Rachel in a thoughtful voice. "He's acting like a pig. Treating him like a foal won't do any good. We have to think of something a pig would want—like acorns."

"You're right," said Penelope.

She waved her wand, and a big basket of acorns appeared on the ground below. While Jack Frost was still trying to get Frisky to play with the stuffed toy, the three fairies zoomed downward and hid behind a nearby hay bale.

Kirsty watched Frisky as he stared at
the acorns.

"Come on," she whispered, hardly
daring to breathe in case it frightened
him away. "Come on, Frisky."

Frisky took one step toward them . . .
and then another. Then he trotted over
to the acorns and started nibbling. But
Jack Frost was close behind him. The Ice
Lord scooped Frisky up into his arms and
squeezed him tightly.

"I've got another surprise for you," he

bellowed at the little foal.

"Oh, poor
Frisky," said
Penelope.

Jack Frost
lifted Frisky's
ear and
whispered
into it, "I've
built you a new
home."

He strode
away from the acorn basket, carrying
Frisky. The three fairies darted high into
the air and followed him as he tramped
away from the Ice Castle. He walked
past frozen fountains and snow-covered
shrubs until he reached a little huddle of
weeping willows, stiff with frost.

"Close your eyes," Jack Frost told Frisky.

Frisky oinked again, his eyes wide open. Jack Frost waved his wand, and the weeping willows parted their branches like curtains. Inside, the girls saw a foal-sized version of the Ice Castle. It was guarded by tiny goblin statues, and Jack Frost clapped his hands together in delight.

"It looks cleaner and tidier than the real thing," Rachel whispered.

The windows sparkled, and when they peered through, the fairies could see that the little castle looked dry and bright. There were blue curtains at every window and the wooden drawbridge had been polished until it gleamed.

"Welcome to your new home," said Jack Frost. "The drawbridge really works."

He put Frisky down and watched him run into the castle. Then he closed the drawbridge, and the fairies heard a furious oink and squeal from the little foal. The next moment, Frisky came sailing over the castle wall and past the moat. Then he began to snuffle at the ground like a pig looking for food.

"Frisky, stop!" Jack Frost roared.

Kirsty turned to Rachel and Penelope with an excited look on her face. Seeing Frisky snuffling like a pig had given her an idea.

"I've got a plan," she whispered. "I think I know how we can get Frisky back."

# A Spell and a Splash

As quickly as she could, Kirsty explained
her plan. She thought that for anyone to
get close to Frisky, the foal needed to be
relaxed—but the only way for him to feel
relaxed was if he was treated like a pig.
As soon as they heard the plan, Rachel

and Penelope started to smile.

"Good thinking, Kirsty," Rachel said.

Penelope raised her wand and spoke the words of a spell.

*"Frisky thinks that he's a pig.*
*So we'll lay a trail of acorns big!*
*Then we'll find a game a foal will enjoy,*
*And he'll be such a happy boy!"*

Instantly, a trail of golden fairy dust whooshed out of the wand tip and swirled

across the garden to an open lawn. There it hopped across the grass, placing an acorn wherever it touched the ground. At the far

end of the lawn was a slope leading to a
big, muddy ditch. Kirsty and Rachel smiled.

"That's perfect for Frisky," said Rachel.

Frisky spotted the acorns at once and
oinked with delight. He rushed toward
them, snuffling. He started to gobble
them up. Jack Frost stumbled after him,
waving his arms and shouting. Frisky
took absolutely no notice. He was having
a wonderful time.

Jack Frost kept on running, trying to catch the little foal. Penelope, Rachel, and Kirsty fluttered above the last acorn.

"Get ready to catch Frisky as soon as he reaches us," said Kirsty.

The foal gobbled up the last acorn and the fairies zoomed down to catch him. But Jack Frost was close behind, and he flew through the air, snatching Frisky and splashing down into the muddy ditch below. *SPLOOSH!* Mucky water shot

into the air
and drenched
the fairies'
delicate wings,
bringing them all
tumbling down
into the ditch.
Frisky squirmed
away from Jack
Frost as the fairies started to wade out of
the ditch, shaking mud from their wings.

"Frisky, it's me," Penelope said.

Frisky looked confused, and tried to run
away. But his little hooves slipped in the
mud and he slid sideways, knocking all
the fairies over again. Jack Frost clawed
his way toward the foal. Then he slipped
and fell flat on his face in the mud.

"This way, Frisky!" Kirsty said.

"Over here," Jack Frost called, wiping mud from his eyes.

The foal darted sideways and the Ice Lord managed to catch him. But Frisky squirmed away again, sending a spray of mud into Jack Frost's open mouth. As Jack Frost sputtered, Frisky ran into the waiting arms of Kirsty and Rachel.

Penelope flew to the magical foal's

side and gave
him a gentle
cuddle. He gave
a little snorting
noise and snuggled
closer to her. He
snuffled . . .
and then he
let out a loud,
horsey neigh.

Rachel, Kirsty, and Penelope
exchanged delighted smiles as Frisky
whinnied with joy.

"He's back to being a normal foal
again," said Rachel. "Well, a normal
magical foal."

"Now we just have to persuade him to
get out of the mud," said Penelope with
a laugh.

"Let's get *ourselves* out of the mud first," said Kirsty, gazing down at her dirty jeans and T-shirt. "It's lucky we were wearing our oldest clothes."

Laughing, they helped one another out of the mud, holding on to Frisky to make sure that he didn't scamper off again. Then Penelope waved her wand, and instantly their clothes were clean and dry once more.

"Aren't you forgetting someone?" Jack Frost hissed, crawling out of the ditch on his hands and knees. "This is all your fault."

His clothes were soaked. His spiky hair

was dripping with globs of mud. Even his eyelids had mud on them. He stood up and glared at Penelope.

"Give him back to me," he demanded.

"You know I'm not going to do that," said Penelope in her gentle voice.

"I've lost the duckling, the lamb, and the foal," Jack Frost wailed. "How am I going to have a petting zoo now?"

"They weren't yours to begin with," said Kirsty.

"It's not fair," Jack Frost complained, slumping down onto the grass. "Everyone's so mean to me. No one wants me."

Just then, Rachel noticed something moving out of the corner of her eye. She turned and saw that Snowdrop and the mother snow goose had followed Jack

Frost as fast as their little legs could carry them. Now they were gazing at him with longing expressions.

"It's not true that no one wants you," Rachel said. "You're just not looking in the right place."

But Jack Frost wasn't in the mood to listen. He got up and stomped away with a grumpy expression. The snow geese followed him, and the girls sighed.

"I hope that he starts paying attention to them again soon," said Kirsty. "I want them to be happy, just like Penelope and Frisky."

"As soon as the magical farm babies are back where they belong, I'm sure Jack Frost will notice the snow geese again," said Penelope.

"That's another good reason to find

the last missing animal," said Rachel. "Everyone should be with their pets, just like you and Frisky."

Kirsty nodded. "All pets deserve to be as happy as Frisky!"

# True Friends

Penelope smiled at Frisky. He was still rolling around in the ditch.

"Things are starting to get back to normal," she said. "Now I need to take Frisky back to the Fluttering Fairyland Farm."

"Farmer Francis will be so glad to see him," said Kirsty.

"He'll be very happy," said Penelope. "But before I can return him, I need to take you two back to Greenfields Farm."

She held out her arms, and Rachel and Kirsty shared a hug with her.

"Thank you for helping me find Frisky," she said. "Thank you with all my heart."

"We're so happy to be able to help you and the other Farm Animal Fairies," said Rachel.

Penelope smiled and raised her wand. Everything around Rachel and Kirsty seemed to shimmer and blur. Then they were surrounded by lush green grass. The four horses in the paddock were still there. But the foals were no longer rolling around in the squishy mud, squealing and snorting like piglets—they were back in the paddock where they belonged, frisking around. The horses looked on as the little foals played together.

"Well, they seem to be having lots of fun," said Kirsty, laughing.

"It's so good to see them back to normal again," said Rachel.

"Yes," Kirsty agreed. "But they do look rather grubby. Let's give them baths and groom them so they're ready for the photo shoot."

The girls hurried back to the gate and collected their buckets of soapy water. Then  they caught the playful foals and washed each one nice and clean before brushing their coats and manes until they gleamed.

"Now we have to get their photos taken before they get dirty again," said Rachel, clipping a halter around each foal's neck.

"Harriet said that they would wait for us in the barn," said Kirsty, gathering up the grooming equipment.

They hurried to the barn and found Blossom still standing outside. She gave a loud moo as she watched the girls lead the foals into the barn. Harriet and Niall were inside setting up a camera.

"We've made a lovely play area for them," said Niall when he saw the girls. "Wow, they have never looked cleaner. Come on, foals."

Harriet and Niall took lots of photos for the website and posters as the little foals played and frisked around together.

Rachel and Kirsty watched the photo shoot, and even Blossom wandered in to find out what was going on.

In the farmhouse that evening, the girls sat down around the kitchen table with Mr. and Mrs. Tate. Harriet and Niall were holding the new poster between them.

"I can't wait to see it," said Rachel, squeezing her best friend's hand.

Smiling, Harriet and Niall laid the new poster out on the table. Everyone smiled at the funny photos of the foals.

"It's perfect," said Mr. Tate. "The poster looks great and the photos will bring visitors flocking to the farm."

"The girls did a wonderful job of grooming the foals," said Harriet. "One of them is so clean that it's almost as if it's sparkling."

Kirsty and Rachel leaned over and looked closer at the picture.

"The foal *is*

sparkling," Kirsty whispered in Rachel's ear. "It's *Frisky*. How did he get on the poster?"

"It must be fairy magic," Rachel replied.

It was good to know that Frisky was safe. But they also knew that they couldn't relax yet. Their fairy friends still had to get one more magical farm animal back.

"Billie can trust us to help bring Chompy home," said Kirsty. "We won't let Jack Frost turn tomorrow's

grand opening into a disaster."

The girls exchanged a secret smile.

"You're right," said Rachel. "The Farm Animal Fairies can depend on us—and so can Greenfields Farm!"

RAINBOW
magic
THE Farm Animal FAIRIES

Rachel and Kirsty have found Debbie's, Elodie's,
and Penelope's missing magic animals.
Now it's time for them to help

# Billie
the Baby Goat Fairy!

Join their next adventure in this
special sneak peek . . .

# A Big Day and a Big Problem

The sun was shining brightly on Greenfields Farm, and the fresh early-morning breeze made it the perfect spring day. Butterflies and bees were already busy around the flowers and bushes. Rachel Walker and her best friend, Kirsty Tate, were walking away from the farmhouse, feeling a very special kind of excitement.

"The big day has finally arrived," said Kirsty, pausing to take a long, deep breath of fresh country air. "I can't wait for the grand opening to start!"

The girls—together with Kirsty's parents—had been staying at the farm during spring break to help the Tates' friends, Harriet and Niall Hawkins, get the farm ready to welcome visitors.

"I want to be sure that everything is perfect," said Rachel.

The girls had been given the very special job of looking after the baby farm animals. They had loved every minute of it, and this morning they had woken up extra early so that they could check on all the baby animals before the grand opening.

"Let's visit the ducklings first," said Kirsty.

They walked past the barn and along the winding path that led to the duck pond. As soon as they had walked between the trees, they saw the glittering water of the pond, with its tall cattails and its happy ducks. Lots of little ducklings were quacking as they splashed around.

"They all look fine," said Rachel. "Shall we check the lambs next? I love the way they bounce around when they see us. It's as if they've got springs in their hooves."

In the sheep pasture, the lambs bounced just as lambs should, and Rachel and

Kirsty gave them some food and patted their fluffy white wool. Their eager baaing made the girls smile.

"Foals next," said Kirsty. "I wonder if they will still be clean after the bath we gave them yesterday?"

"No way," said Rachel, laughing. "You know how much they love rolling in all those muddy puddles."

Sure enough, when they arrived at the stables, they found all the foals coated in mud, neighing happily as they rolled and splashed.

"I'm so glad they're all OK," said Kirsty. "Thank goodness Jack Frost and his pesky goblins haven't caused any more trouble."

"At least not yet," said Rachel.

# RAINBOW magic™

# Which Magical Fairies Have You Met?

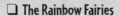

- ❏ The Rainbow Fairies
- ❏ The Weather Fairies
- ❏ The Jewel Fairies
- ❏ The Pet Fairies
- ❏ The Sports Fairies
- ❏ The Ocean Fairies
- ❏ The Princess Fairies
- ❏ The Superstar Fairies
- ❏ The Fashion Fairies
- ❏ The Sugar & Spice Fairies
- ❏ The Earth Fairies
- ❏ The Magical Crafts Fairies
- ❏ The Baby Animal Rescue Fairies
- ❏ The Fairy Tale Fairies
- ❏ The School Day Fairies
- ❏ The Storybook Fairies
- ❏ The Friendship Fairies

**■ SCHOLASTIC**

Find all of your favorite fairy friends at
**scholastic.com/rainbowmagic**

RMFAIRY17

SPECIAL EDITION

# Which Magical Fairies Have You Met?

- ❏ Joy the Summer Vacation Fairy
- ❏ Holly the Christmas Fairy
- ❏ Kylie the Carnival Fairy
- ❏ Stella the Star Fairy
- ❏ Shannon the Ocean Fairy
- ❏ Trixie the Halloween Fairy
- ❏ Gabriella the Snow Kingdom Fairy
- ❏ Juliet the Valentine Fairy
- ❏ Mia the Bridesmaid Fairy
- ❏ Flora the Dress-Up Fairy
- ❏ Paige the Christmas Play Fairy
- ❏ Emma the Easter Fairy
- ❏ Cara the Camp Fairy
- ❏ Destiny the Rock Star Fairy
- ❏ Belle the Birthday Fairy
- ❏ Olympia the Games Fairy
- ❏ Selena the Sleepover Fairy

- ❏ Cheryl the Christmas Tree Fairy
- ❏ Florence the Friendship Fairy
- ❏ Lindsay the Luck Fairy
- ❏ Brianna the Tooth Fairy
- ❏ Autumn the Falling Leaves Fairy
- ❏ Keira the Movie Star Fairy
- ❏ Addison the April Fool's Day Fairy
- ❏ Bailey the Babysitter Fairy
- ❏ Natalie the Christmas Stocking Fairy
- ❏ Lila and Myla the Twins Fairies
- ❏ Chelsea the Congratulations Fairy
- ❏ Carly the School Fairy
- ❏ Angelica the Angel Fairy
- ❏ Blossom the Flower Girl Fairy
- ❏ Skyler the Fireworks Fairy
- ❏ Giselle the Christmas Ballet Fairy
- ❏ Alicia the Snow Queen Fairy

**■SCHOLASTIC**

3 stories in each one!

HIT entertainment

Find all of your favorite fairy friends at
**scholastic.com/rainbowmagic**

RMSPECIAL20